Not Jun...

Written by Clare Helen Welsh

Illustrated by Irene Montano

Collins

This is Zap.

Zap picks up junk.

4

The fox is not junk.

Zap has a shell.

6

The shell is not junk.

Is this a laptop?

Is this a ship?

12

The box is not junk.

After reading

Letters and Sounds: Phase 3

Word count: 40

Focus phonemes: /nk/ /th/ /z/ /x/ /sh/ /y/

Common exception words: no, the

Curriculum links: Understanding the World, People and Communities

Early learning goals: Reading: read and understand simple sentences; use phonic knowledge to decode regular words and read them aloud accurately; read some common irregular words; demonstrate understanding when talking with others about what they have read

Developing fluency

- Model reading the speech bubbles with expression. Ask: How could you say these words differently?
- Encourage your child to sound talk and then blend the words e.g. j/u/nk. It may help to point to each sound as your child reads.
- Then ask your child to reread the sentence to support fluency and understanding.

Phonic practice

- Ask your child to sound talk and blend each of the following words: f/o/x, sh/e/ll, sh/i/p, b/o/x, j/u/nk.
- Ask your child to say the words that have a /sh/ sound in: chop, ship, duck, sink, posh, fish, shock, shell. (*ship, posh, fish, shock, shell*)
- Look at the "I spy sounds" pages (14–15). Discuss the picture with your child. Can they find items/ examples of words with the /x/ and /nk/ sounds in? (*fox, box, mix, axe, six, tank, sink, junk, drink*)

Extending vocabulary

- Ask your child:
  o What words could you use instead of **junk**? (e.g. *rubbish, litter, scrap, jumble, recycling, waste*)
  o What noises/sounds do you think the robot might make? (e.g. *zap, zip, beep, clunk*)